A step in the direction of

Zerth
UNWINDING

Rubin Walter: Danger to the Max

by Mighty Rahiem

© 2018 Nate Cornick

ISBN-13: 978-0-9998398-1-2

Cover and illustrations by Mighty Rahiem

Introduction

by

Gustav D. Gustav

A good friend once told me, any thinking man (or woman, for all that it matters) will, under the right circumstances, categorize his existence in the grand scheme of things and inevitably find himself annoyed. Such is the sentiment of a man in servitude, for any sincere pondering on the matter would reveal that lines have somehow become crossed and now resemble more of a web than anything productive. Such is the life of most humans – wound up, annoyed and constricted by the web they have allowed themselves to entertain. Understanding such a state is the purpose of the Zerth.

My name is Gustav D. Gustav and I am a Human. I make the distinction because it's necessary that I clarify, given my current situation. I write this introduction with the intent of enriching the lives of those who have found themselves bound-up and retarded by their own aspirations, as an alternative is available to those who are willing to take the plunge. For those amenable to entertain what might best be described as a surrogate existence (which is how I prefer to think of it), a vast system has been established, allowing the willing to unmask their true potential and fully realize their intended state.

Now, when I say 'intended state', this is all conjecture, but it would be dishonest of me to omit my own personal bias, as I feel that I can comment on the situation with some authority. You see, though only 42 years of age, I have experienced over 60 years of consciousness. Now that the naysayers and professional skeptics are out of the way, allow me to explain in terms you might best accept.

There is a place I hang my heart, far away from the hazards and horrors of earthly life, where the soul is free to wander and flourish – taking root within the fertile soil of limitless imagination and blossoming wild into whatever form one's restless heart desires. Fantasy? Most certainly, but I assure you, that word has no bearing on its authenticity.

Picture a world where the sun never sets, the beer never goes flat and there's always room at the table for more. Imagine dashing in front of a speeding bus and being flattened, only to return to laugh at the horrified distortion of your own lips as they've been peeled over your own battered face. Envision an ocean of uncharted mystery and a sky, just as accessible as the car in your driveway, all a quick step from your front door. Imagine building your dream home as quickly as you can dream it, and the materials are plentiful and free. And picture a wealth of relationships – family and friends of all kinds, all trusting and willing to share in the experience. Is it paradise? I would say so, but most are content to call it Zerth.

I call this place home because I was only born on Earth once, whereas Zerth has granted me dozens of opportunities to draw my first breath. As I digress, Bill Murray makes the case that repetitive suicide would inevitably result in boredom – I can personally attest to the opposite. All grim fantasy aside, consider this introduction to be my way of opening the door for you. I've been told that my writing lacks a certain amount of warmth (which I acknowledge), so in the interest of bringing more excitement into the narrative, I've asked those closest to me to dictate the following works in their own words. I urge you to take whatever you can from its contents and allow it to cultivate the infinite within your own mind – after all, *you* are what it's all about.

Mighty Rahiem

Rubin Walter jumped cows for a living. At least that's what he told strangers who wondered how he could afford such an expensive bike. When asked if cow-jumping was good business, he inevitably scurried off in search of more gullible company. Fort Valley, Georgia had plenty of cows and plenty of gullible company, but the occasional smart-ass would creep in to ruin his mood.

Rubin didn't need to finish High School. There were no courses on ramp-building or pulling wheelies, so he dropped out after Intro to Mechanics. Everything else was just filler. He was offered a job bagging groceries at Harvey's Supermarket but quit when it took too much time away from his riding schedule. He had his future to focus on and he wasn't about to let the present get in the way.

It was July of 1988 when Rubin Walter graduated to jumping over cars. There was still no money in it but he knew the payday was right around the corner – he could feel it. Each Volvo and

Oldsmobile that passed beneath his tires was one step closer to the big time. It didn't bother him that people said he was a loser, or that he wasn't going anywhere with his life; his girl Amy was the winner of the Peach County Princess contest and she thought he was just fine. Didn't matter that she had won it when she was 12, she was still his princess.

In August of 1990, Rubin and Amy got married. It was a small ceremony in the dirt lot where Rubin worked, but there were flowers and Def Leppard presided over the event to the tune of *Pour Some Sugar on Me*. The cows were in attendance, as well as Amy's father, who was glad he was only on the hook for the cost of a bouquet and a Sanyo M-W20F. Together, Rubin and Amy carved out a little patch of heaven amongst the dust and abandoned cars.

With Amy's help, Rubin amassed a small following of loyal fans. He built a set of bleachers for the audience, though it was a debate whether they were loyal to Rubin or to the stolen kegs of Keystone Light that were stationed around the place. Whatever it took to keep butts in seats. Over time, some even stuck around to cheer Rubin on when he took a tumble. It wasn't ideal, but Rubin had no reason to complain. They all remembered his name.

In August of 1991, Rubin took a spill and his bike rolled into a crowd of 12 shrieking fans, catching Amy in the back of the neck and killing her. It made the news. 'Local Daredevil kills wife'. Rubin was devastated. His girl, his bike and his life, gone with one little slip-up. He was even arrested for it but his public defender got him off as long as Rubin told the judge that he wasn't really a daredevil. He was legally obligated to admit he was a loser – and with that, he was lost. In April of 1992, Rubin went to sleep in the passenger seat of a 1985 Pontiac Firebird and didn't wake up. At least, he didn't wake up on Earth. He was found unconscious with fingers dug into the ivory sands of Bonzo Beach.

Rubin was hoisted to his feet by something that looked like an insect and given a hearty pat on the back, as well as a crumpled letter addressed to "Mr. Human". Upon reading the note, he was instructed to return it to the insect and deposit himself into the flatbed of a flying pickup truck. When he refused, he found himself unconscious in the flatbed of a flying pickup truck.

Rubin awoke to the familiar buzz of construction. He was propped up and offered his first paycheck in the form of an envelope containing what looked like a credit card. He was instructed to build a house, and upon completion, one hundred bucks would be added to his card. One hundred bucks to build a house. The insects seemed to be running the operation, along with another Human named Anthony. When he asked if he was in hell, the reply was "Yer on Zerth, buddy. Pick up a shovel and get used to it."

Rubin declined the offer and wandered around for a few days, kicking rocks and getting friendly with the locals; the strangest creatures he had ever seen. They were like something from a tame cartoon nightmare. A little lizard thing named Kix – looking like a green banana with arms – followed him around, chirping like a bird. A towering clod of fuzz by the name of Harie claimed to be a woman, and offered him money for sex; and a talking turnip stole his wallet and disappeared into the setting of a dozen suns.

They weren't all bad. The Sectoids, as they called themselves, seemed quite inviting. Sure, they looked like the centerpiece of a Whitley Strieber novel, and maybe they did smell like Vaseline, but their general haughtiness brought his memories back to good old Fort Valley. And their big black bug eyes cast a perfect reflection of his precious pompadour.

One particular Sectoid, by the name of Hesh, seemed real friendly. Hesh showed Rubin the ropes as far as scavenging was concerned, and together the two went into business scouring the sands for scraps worth selling. It was during this time that Rubin was introduced to the Hyperbike. The goddamned thing could float and it had no wheels! It looked like half a blue watermelon with a chair behind it – and big sticks flying out the back. But the sound it made sent Ruben to his knees, weeping like a God-struck Baptist.

Determining horsepower was impossible, as there was no torque involved. The engine was some kind of magnet derived spinning module… or something. There was nothing usual about the construction, as far as Rubin was concerned, but with a bit of effort, he grew to understand the machines as well as his beloved bike back home.

Magenite cores in the center of heat regulating fans kept the bike afloat. Heat distributors passed through the cores, powered by simple wires from the battery, much like an electric stove top. Balance was maintained using the nav-system in the dash-board between the drive handles, and the head-fan in front kept the whole thing moving forward. The blades of the fan were tipped with Magenite and rapid micro-bursts of electricity pulled the blades along. The harder you pushed the throttle, the more rapid the sparks. Blinkbottom 6, they called it. The sixth generation of head-fans developed by the world-famous Blinkbottom Industries.

The Blinkbottom 6 was capable of accelerating to unfathomable speeds. Roughly 8000 rpm. Rear stabilizers kept the bike moving straight and allowed for the bike to turn, rotating the stabilizers in whatever direction you wanted to go using the foot pedals. Thrust was achieved by twisting the throttle, just like a motorcycle, which regulated the speed of the head-fan. The break system was a dream. No grinding or smashing or pressure or anything; only reverse motion. The break handle regulated the speed of the break-fan which rotated in the opposite direction while the head-fan slowed to a halt.

No belts, no oil pan, no gas. All electric and all so simple. Zero to sixty in less than three seconds and sixty to zero in only twice that – unless ya hit something. Even better, the gravity of the planet was a bit less than that on Earth, making the jumps even bigger and the tumbles not nearly as painful. Rubin had found his new love.

Rubin's other new love, a Sectoid girl named Chelli, was too damned tall. She towered over his 5'6" frame at a domineering 6'2". Though she didn't consider him a match, she plagued his dreams with all her bouncing bits and silkiness. And that smile, and those hips! Didn't matter that she didn't have a nose or ears, Rubin lusted after her with every bit of his eager loins. Not just her, but all the bug girls. They all oozed sexy. But no, Chelli was head-deep into Hesh like a nerd in a swirly. He just couldn't fathom why the girl bugs were so much bigger than the boys.

On the other side of the spectrum, the damned Morouni girls couldn't be told apart from the guys, minus the bulbous fuzzy boobs, of course. The Legomi didn't have girls, apparently, and neither did the Sluggs.

Not that it mattered, there was nothing appealing about a walking carrot, or gibbering lizard-thing.

On the topic of Human women, Rubin found most, if not all Human girls to be rugged and crazy. Almost like being a nut was a prerequisite to be… wherever they were. But then again, so were all the guys. Still, none came close to his girl back home. He would talk about Amy like she was still alive and not mangled in a casket. It was no one's business to know the truth.

Rubin Walter spent his time on Zerth with his attention buried in polarite actuators, head-fan housings and Chelli's cleavage. It wasn't long before he attempted his first jump in front of a crowd of nearly 100. There were no cows around, but there were macromites. Lumbering cow-sized mites that looked more like a boulder than anything else. No eyes, no ears, no head. Just a big flubby body with a snout and six legs like tree trunks. They were docile as hell – you could shoot one and it wouldn't even know it. The bullet would just disappear into the skin. Some people tried using them for clearing land, but their rows ended up looping all around and zigzagging. Despite the beasts being so calm, they were impossible to control. Walking in a straight line was not an option and any kind of barrier you tried to put in its way would get run over. Lining up more than one at a time was not worth the effort, so Rubin was content to jump just the one.

Rubin's daring antics quickly earned him some credit around the work-site and he started collecting donations with each jump; something he never got back in Georgia. Despite being hellish to look at, most of the people of Zerth were beyond friendly – and not that southern kind of friendly – real friendly. No one talked out the side of their mouth or hid their intentions behind lying lips. They all genuinely liked him and he genuinely liked Zerth. There was no such thing as a loser there; everyone was a winner and failure was not an option because there was nothing to fail at. If your house fell over you got to build a new one – better than the last one. Need materials? Go pick some up, it's all free. Need a new battery for the bike? Draw a stick figure for the talking onion and he will eat it up, literally, and give you a battery in return.

Communication was another marvel. The Sectoids had crates upon crates of wrist-watch style communication devices that worked just like a telephone, a map and a bank account all in one. They called it a Talkman. Price tag: five bucks. Upon activation, you would be asked to enter your desired code-number specific to yourself. That number became your identity. The constant rotation of the suns acted as communication satellites, bouncing the signal around. Anyone could dial in your number and have a conversation with you anywhere on the planet. Rubin's number was 1281990, the day he got married. Everyone knew Rubin's number and he delighted in talking with anyone who cared to listen. Especially the

Legomi, who seemed to get a kick out of calling him from three feet away behind a rock. It never got old to them, and neither did his stories.

As far as Earthly materials were concerned, death was big business. It seemed that killing yourself could be quite lucrative. Men and women would blow their brains out and return from the dead a few minutes later with a spare tire or a new gun, or more ammo. For Rubin, every tumble on his bike was a new opportunity to head home for supplies. If the bike didn't kill him, he had a handy hand-cannon to finish the job, thanks to Larry Beagle.

Larry Beagle ran Beagle's Deagles, and he made more money than anyone. Larry had the good fortune of owning a .50 caliber Desert Eagle pistol. He would sell them for fifty bucks a pop; driving up river with a buyer and returning a few hours later with a duplicate firearm and a very happy customer. He would let them shoot him with their new gun and he would show up again with a duplicate. It was great, clean fun. Hell of a way to earn a living.

Given Rubin's hobby of vehicular carnage, he and Larry found themselves working together and the two became close friends. Larry would get blown away and Rubin would ramp over his corpse to wild applause. Along with Hesh and Chelli, the four traveled the world, putting on shows for the local population. The events were funded by Larry's bulging wallet and he would often come out the other side with a lot more to show for all the work. Donations flooded in and their fame grew. Rubin Walter – Danger to the Max. They even printed up a banner with his name on it.

Maybe his work routinely killed him, but Rubin didn't mind; for the first time in his life, he had an audience. Sure, they were lizard-things and turnips and freaks, but the love was real. Even the other Humans got a kick out of his antics, calling him the Evel Knievel of Zerth. Every day, Rubin pushed his dreams farther, and after a few years, he had earned himself somewhat of a celebrity status. He jumped buses and rivers and houses; he even considered jumping Aerie Tower, but was shot at when scouting the location.

After six years in business, Rubin was convinced he was in heaven. The world was creeping to life around him and new Humans were spawning in every day; each with their own unique brand of crazy. The fishers would bring them into town and offer them work, just like they had done with him so many years before.

One day, as Rubin sat snacking on barbecue rat lion haunch, a vision of pure beauty flashed before his eyes. She shuffled through town with frizzed hair and that all-too-familiar "I'm in hell" look on her face. Her name was Lisa and she was from Florida, 2011. A girl from the future! Rubin was hooked. Together Lisa and Rubin spent their time cooking, ramping over shit and chatting about Earth. Lisa filled Rubin in on the decades he missed and Rubin showed her the clean, Zerth-style living that he had grown to love.

Strangely, Lisa wasn't even born at the time that Ruben spawned in, which made for some strange conversation; especially since Lisa was quite obviously in her early twenties and Ruben hadn't seemed to have aged a day in eight years – no matter. After two years, Lisa and Rubin got married. Married meaning they told everyone they were married, as there was no religious structure or beliefs whatsoever. If it was good enough for the Sectoids, it was good enough for them. Still, they weren't about to tie the knot without fanfare.

Rubin wanted a big show of the event and had his eyes on the winding Georgio Gorge. The canyon cut through the pebbled red-rock flats like a luge; an upended omega gash that snaked through the coastal terrain like a big bent pipe. Hesh recommended Rubin settle for jumping the town of Ender, which he said was a more realistic goal. It sat just off to the side of the gorge – kind of a dry-land estuary into the greater ravine. You wouldn't even see it from the plains above, as the whole town was hidden in the winding passages below.

It took some convincing to keep Rubin's attention away from the gorge itself, as the shortest distance to cross was nearly 500 feet of air, so Rubin settled for the pocket over the town. A 270 foot jump.

The ceremony was a joyous affair. There was no practice run or calculating trajectory; this was Rubin's big day and he wasn't about to let that kind of stress bring him down. Hesh hired a DJ who had all of Def Leppard's albums, and Chelli set up a broadcast tower to beam the event across the whole planet. It was a big hit. As fireworks exploded above, Rubin tumbled down with a flash of inspiration. He didn't care what Hesh said – one day, he would jump the Georgio Gorge.

Though Rubin didn't survive his wedding, the reception was a raucous two-day parade across Anu Bardus, finally meeting up with the reborn groom at the banks of the Pareggi River. Rubin scooped up his bride and rushed her away for a honeymoon aboard a lumbering Morouni steamer. A week-long trek across the wastes, fully catered with an open bar. Rubin didn't survive the alcohol, so there was a brief stop in Bonzo Beach where the groom was delivered to Lisa by a pair of tuxedoed fishers.

It was the ideal Zertian wedding and it bumped Rubin's name to the front of everyone's attention. His audience grew like wildfire. Donations flooded in, and a few weeks later, Rubin and Lisa bought a house. A 3 bedroom dobi overlooking the grand Pareggi; open munda so Lisa could trim the vines. Together, the two had a son. Rocket was his name.

All his life, Rubin wished that his father had named him something with more spunk to it. Something edgy and defiant. He tried several names throughout his career but nothing stuck, and he wasn't about to let the same mistake be repeated. His son was going to be just like him and he would have a proper name fitting of a death-defying showman. Rocket Walter was born on Jubai 35th, of the year 112, the same year the town of Ghong was made legit. Ghong was the first real town established in the region, and Rocket Walter was the first Human born there. It wasn't long after that Larry Beagle had a daughter of his own. Lilly was her name and the two toddlers were inseparable.

It was the perfect home for a new family. There were no shortages of friends for Rocket and Lilly to play with and everyone treated them like their own. While Rubin and Larry were away jumping over things and getting shot, Lisa and the rest of the town watched over the children. The daredevil would come home after a long day of gravity induced trauma and greet his family with kisses and hugs and money. It was truly heaven for Rubin, and he had no intention of ever leaving that place behind.

In the month of Gary in the year 119, Rocket shot Lilly dead. The 7 year old was sent to his room without supper, as Rubin had warned him to stay away from his gun collection. The whole town got together at Bonzo Beach to wait for Lilly's return, but she didn't show up. They tried again in Azura, but no one had seen a 7 year old girl falling from the sky. They looked in Tarqus and the Gravity fields, but there was no sign of the girl. Wanted signs were plastered around pubs and Fisher-kings were interrogated, but it was no use – Lilly just didn't come back.

Larry didn't take the news well at all. Lilly was his little sunshine and now she was gone. No one knew how to explain it, but the theory rolled around that, since Lilly didn't exist on Earth, she had no place to go back to when she died. She was a native and therefore wasn't afforded the benefit of respawning. It made sense. Humans didn't age on Zerth, so how could a child be brought into the world without being stuck in a newborn body?

It was determined that Natives of Zerth were governed by a different set of rules than everyone else. Sunborn, they called them, and they were sheltered by terrified parents. How could such a fragile being exist in such a hostile place? What a curse. From that moment on, Rubin abandoned any hope for Rocket's future as a daredevil. If death was permanent for his son, there was no way he could carry on his legacy. It was just too dangerous.

As for Rocket, the boy was as confused as anyone could be. He thought he was just having fun, as he had seen uncle Larry get shot a dozen times to the laughter and applause of everyone around. But when he did it, everyone stopped talking to him. Beyond all that, Lilly was gone and it was his fault. Nobody blamed him for her death, but nobody talked about it either. Even as a child, Rocket knew he had messed up.

But the show must go on. Rubin continued performing for thousands; though Larry's business took a turn. After Lilly's death, Larry changed; he wasn't so gung-ho about dying anymore. Not that he was overcome by depression or anything like that; more like he just slowed down. He smiled differently in those days; a deeper smile – more genuine it seemed.

Larry talked about how his time on Earth was getting longer and longer, and he felt like he was having to dwell on certain things just to get back to Zerth – things he didn't like thinking about. He said it felt like he had to take a step backwards and get all wound up in the past, and only then could he come back.

Larry talked about how he thought Zerth was really just a dream for people with problems; a place for the disturbed to act out their fantasies so they could learn more about themselves. When they got over it, they didn't need the dream anymore so they stopped showing up. Rubin didn't buy it. His fantasies were alive and well and he always came back. Larry said it's because he was ignoring something.

The next time Larry died he came back much older. He looked like he had aged 20 years. His hair was gray and he had a certain sparkle in his eye. He kept telling everyone that he missed them so much and was so happy to see everyone again, but for the people of Zerth, he was only gone for a few minutes.

For Larry, it had been much longer. He said that he and his wife had adopted and raised a child and had been working as a welder in Montana, but had since retired. He assured everyone that he would stay on Zerth as long as he lived, but he wouldn't be coming back again if he died. Rubin didn't believe him at first, but the look in Larry's eyes didn't lie. He looked like he had found heaven.

A few weeks later, Rubin met the day with a chirp from his Talkman. It was Larry Beagle transferring 8 million bucks to his account. His whole life savings. Rubin hurried to Larry's office where he found his friend's body on the floor with a bullet in his head. He had seen his friend like that a thousand times before, but something was different. He didn't know how to explain it, but there was an emptiness in his chest. Among Larry's things was a carefully drafted note addressed to Rubin.

To my friend Rubin.

I want to thank you for helping me find meaning in so many lives. I want to thank you for all the memories and all the good times, and I want to thank you for never letting go.

But most of all, I want to thank you for the flowers.

It's been a hell of a ride and I wouldn't trade a minute of it for anything.

Your friend always,

Larry Beagle.

The note was too much and the questions piled up in Rubin's mind. Larry's lifeless eyes gazed up to the ceiling, filled with stars, and that was the last time Rubin saw his friend.

Rubin was in a panic; first, his son, now his friend. He didn't know what to do. Without warning, his entire life was falling apart around him.

Everything he counted on was being ripped away and he found himself cursing the suns for taking away everything he loved. All around he saw his beloved Zerth falling apart. Sunborn children were showing up every day and people were insisting they stop killing each other. Do it for the children, they said. His faith in immortality was being challenged. This wasn't the Zerth he loved and he felt torn between two worlds – revel in danger and risk his family, or give up his dreams to keep them safe. It was too much for him to take so Rubin put it all out of his head.

Years passed and the show continued. With Larry gone, Rubin pushed himself to the top of his game. He used his inheritance to build stadiums and arenas for crowds of 10,000 or more, and funded research programs into even newer, better hyperbikes. He donated to charities and hospitals to keep Sunborn children healthy and safe; he was becoming a genuine Renaissance man. His face was plastered across billboards and posters and he even had a hot dog named after him. The Walterdog; a hotdog dipped entirely in ketchup. You really needed a fork to eat it, but the fun was getting your face covered in red soupy gore, just like Rubin at the end of his shows. He was a star and his eye was on the biggest prize of all. Soon, he would jump Georgio Gorge, and death could not stand in his way.

In the year 122, Lisa found Rocket in the back lot with a broken leg. The boy had built a wooden ramp and was jumping over trash cans on a minibike. He was wearing a cape with his name on it. When Rubin got home, he found his wounded and teary-eyed son locked in his room by a hysterical wife. For an injury like that, it wasn't uncommon for Rubin to just off himself rather than wait for a bone to heal, but that wasn't an option for Rocket. From that moment on, Rubin knew things had to change. Despite his fame, he stopped putting on shows and focused on raising his son.

For a year, Rubin read to Rocket daily. He took him on trips across the world and introduced him to all the culture Zerth had to offer. They went fishing in the southern seas with Legomi mariners and hiking through the forests of Shishir with Slugg mountaineers – anything to get the boy's mind away from stunt riding. He even took Rocket to see Aerie tower with the Sectoids, but were shot at when scouting the location. But despite Rubin's best efforts, he couldn't escape his fame. No matter where he went, everyone knew him as *the* Rubin Walter – Fearless daredevil. It didn't help that Rocket wanted nothing more than to be just like his father. The boy would ask about Georgio Gorge, to which Rubin was resigned to let it slide. Some dreams just aren't meant to be, he would say. It was a sour lesson for his starry-eyed son.

In truth, Rubin had lost his desire to ride entirely. There was something about the slow life that grasped him and he found himself feeling tired at the thought of riding again. There was so much more to life than performing for a crowd. He had a family now and they needed a patriarch; they needed his care for guidance and stability. Most of all, Rocket needed a real role model that didn't turn-tail and run at the mention of responsibility. He wasn't a daredevil anymore, he was a father, and it didn't bother him one bit.

In Jubai of 123, Rubin was hit by a bus and killed. No big deal. He woke up in the passenger seat of the 1985 Pontiac Firebird the same way he had done a hundred times in the past. It was still August of 1992 and the summer sun was dipping in the sky. He made his way down Vineville St. to Harveys Supermarket for a box of salt to take back to Zerth, as Lisa was running low and wanted to bake some bread for the neighbors. He greeted everyone with a smile and paid for his salt with the last of his pocket change. Rubin returned to the Firebird and waited for sleep to take him home.

Rubin awoke to the morning buzz of cicadas and a wet dew across the windshield. He was still in

Fort Valley. It wasn't panic that overtook him, more of a resolved acceptance. For nearly twenty years, Rubin hadn't seen the day go by, and as he watched a single sun pull over the treetops, he felt a reluctance to return to his adopted home. He was still 19 years old and Harveys Supermarket was still hiring. He didn't care to ramp over shit all day and he didn't even remember that he was a high school dropout. That was another life and Rubin had moved on. He had a hell of a time explaining his newfound maturity to the manager of Harveys when he asked for his old job back.

By November of 1995, Rubin had his own apartment. He was the assistant manager at Harveys and all kinds of women were breaking down the door to be with a young guy making 10 dollars an hour. He could get them discounts on all kinds of great stuff. Despite all the success, the thought of taking yet another wife just made him angry. Though Zerth was behind him, he often found his mind dragged back to his family in good-old Ghong. He knew Rocket didn't miss him. He knew Lisa didn't know he had been gone for so long. If he ever went back, it would be like no time passed at all. The thought left him feeling hollow and he couldn't shake the notion that he wasn't quite finished.

Through the weeks, Rubin was hounded by what should have been his standard routine. One by one, his daily rituals fell away and the effort started to feel wrong – like he was moving backwards. He began to feel an unwillingness to engage in society and his working life took a back seat to wistful thinking; alone under a work lamp with more than enough cigarettes and whiskey. The solitude; he lusted after it. Through days of inventory checks and OSHA reports, Rubin's only concern were the memories of something he walked away from – something he left behind. He just wasn't finished.

Rubin thought back to what Larry told him – that it was all just a dream for disturbed people. The problem was, he wasn't disturbed anymore. Maybe a bit hollow and borderline bitter, but grief was gone for good. That door was closed and he had no intention of revisiting it. He didn't even know how anymore. The void left by his first wife had been filled by something else entirely... something that he was being kept away from. It was his family and Rubin found himself needing it.

Rubin's drinking increased. He drank on the job to dull the ache and he began downing any pills he could get his hands on. Half of him knew what he was doing; the other half just wanted it to end. In short time, Rubin was all wound up and the chaos of it all sparked a familiar flame; a sort of spiked hammer of aggression that he could summon at a moment's notice to beat back any nagging thought of order. He felt like a kid again and he was ready to go home.

Rubin returned to the dirt lot where the Firebird still sat, but it didn't feel right at all. Something about the leather seat felt like he was going backwards. He needed a new entrance; something fitting for death-defying showman. He remembered how the people of Zerth would show up on bicycles and skateboards – as long as it was strapped securely to your person, it would come with you. Hell, one dude even crucified himself to his boat and brought the whole thing along. Strapping himself to his old dirt bike wouldn't be too difficult.

Rubin awoke to a rush of air in his eyes and the outline of blue brickwork. No lungs full of water and no fishers dragging him across the beach. He was falling, belted to his dirt bike in khaki pants and polo shirt. Rubin Walter: Assistant Manager – drunk and twisted and ready for anything. He didn't hesitate to snatch up a Talkman from the fishers and radio for a ride to Ghong. It was like playing an old game and he remembered all the cheat codes. He was in control.

Arriving at Bonzo beach was an odd chore. There were too many questions he didn't care to answer and Lisa was furious that Rubin hadn't brought back any salt. It didn't bother him; Rubin scooped up his family and held them until the memories came rushing back. He almost felt embarrassed to have forgotten so much. He didn't offer any explanation for his sudden compassion and Rocket's comment on the stars in his father's eyes was brushed off as a statement of the obvious. Rubin could see it all clearly; Zerth was not his home, but neither was Earth. His home was nowhere and the thought of it fueled his resolve and pushed him harder than he knew was possible. With that revelation, Rubin prepared for his final act of defiance; his last hurrah. Georgio Gorge.

The following weeks were spent in his office with Hesh, drawing up trajectory calculations and ramp designs. The Sectoid's superior intellect assured Rubin that the deed was impossible – especially with an old rickety dirt bike, but Rubin didn't care. It wasn't about what was possible; it was about what needed to be done. The success of the jump was afterthought and whether he landed safely or in a bloody heap was inconsequential. For Hesh, this was nothing new, but what did strike him as odd was the urgency to draw up plans at all. Rubin never attempted it before, so what was different this time?

Weeks passed and Rubin made the rounds, showing off his Earth-bike and promoting the event. He would rev his gasoline powered combustion engine to the delight of star-struck children and homesick Humans. The Morouni loved it so much they even tried to claim it was their invention. Keeping the thing fueled required a team of suicidal followers, so Rubin dreamed up the idea of having them killed in stunt shows. He would have to take a back seat to the carnage, but his groupies were free to dismember themselves in creative ways to the awe of an adoring public. Once Earthbound, they would be sure to score as many gallons of gasoline as they could in return for a safe ride home and generous weekly wage. Rubin Walter's Maximum Mayhem;

he traveled the planet spreading love, wealth and havoc, all the while generating hype for the final showdown with his greatest prize.

In the month of Garry, in the year 124, Rubin Walter was ready. Millions tuned in to watch the event through a planet-wide broadcast which was beamed into bars and eateries from coast-to-coast. You could even watch it live on the screen of your Talkman, in brilliant 220x176 pseudocolor. It was the event of a lifetime. A live audience of 20,000 gathered in the heat of the Redrock shears above Georgio Gorge to watch Rubin perform his greatest feat. It was reported that the 500 foot jump wasn't possible – especially with Earthtech, but Rubin didn't flinch. Lisa was hysterical. She knew the look in Rubin's eyes and it was impossible to explain to Rocket.

The time had come and Rubin roared into the crowd to thunderous applause as Hesh and his crew of mechanics rushed to the bike for a last minute inspection. All checked out and Rubin gave Hesh a customary fist-bump and he was ready to go. He snapped his goggles to his eyes and zeroed in on his target – a 45 foot long plasteel ramp 300 yards up a dirt path. He gave an assuring thumbs-up to his wife and son, and with that he was off, blasting across the mesa, pushing his engine to the limit. 100Mph – steady and climbing. 200Mph- topping out the gauge as the wind peeled his lips back and whistled through his teeth. Rubin hit the ramp clean and the ground vanished beneath his wheels. That was the last time Rocket saw his father.

Rubin didn't mind Earth so much. It wasn't what it used to be, with all its stigmas and moral obligation. He could handle it pretty well and all the little things just seemed to roll off him like butter off a hot biscuit. He made a decent living at Harvey's but had a habit of confusing customers with stories of his old life. He was a wacky young man who spun yarns that couldn't possibly be true, but it didn't bother too many people. Just an eccentric young man, they said.

Unfortunately for Rubin, his outlandish tales drew the attention of the town shrink. His very vocal recollections of a far-off planet filled with weirdos earned him a one-way ticket to the funny farm, and with it came large blue pills that made the doctors easier to listen to. It wasn't all bad – they were friendly enough and seemed to genuinely want to help him get better. It wasn't too long before the doctors were able to convince him that all his memories were nothing more than vivid dreams and imagination. Despite how real it felt, none of it was true. What *was* real was the guilt of loss over his wife Amy, and it apparently had driven him crazy. Not hard to believe; guilt can really do a man in. With that understanding, he kept on his medication and was allowed to return to work.

The years passed and life returned to normal. Rubin had no urge to revisit his delusions and the old rusted-out Firebird in the lot became nothing more than an embarrassing reminder of his wild years. He tried to sell his bike but no one wanted it – so he pawned it and used the cash for a couple of six-packs and a carton of cigarettes. He made a weekend of it. Flings came and went but he never remarried; it was painful to think about. Too close to home, his shrink said. Best to stay single, and so he did.

After 20 years at Harvey's, Rubin opted for an early retirement. They threw a party for him and they even gave him a watch. He was only 39 when he started drawing from his pension – 812 bucks a month he got, and it was all he needed for a one-bedroom apartment on the east side of town. His old manager told him he could come back any time for the same pay, but Rubin didn't need it. He was happy enough with what he had.

In 2014, Rubin got a phone call from someone he didn't know. A woman by the name of Maryl said that she had found his information on the internet and that she would pay for a greyhound bus ticket if he would come visit her. All the way up in Minnesota. She said her husband was dying and wanted to see his friend before he passed. Apparently, he and Rubin were friends as children and used to ride bikes together growing up, which is something she found hard to believe, given that her husband had never left the state. Rubin didn't know what to say, but took the opportunity to get out of town for a while.

Minnesota was a bit chilly for Rubin's taste, but he had never seen snow before and that alone made the trip worth while. He met Maryl at the station and not much was spoken as she drove him to the Shady Rest retirement home. He didn't quite know how to handle the situation, so he made a quick stop at the gift shop in the entrance and nabbed some flowers. Rubin was introduced to a bed-ridden elderly man who had a hard time hearing, and really didn't speak a word, but the way he smiled when Rubin presented him with a bouquet of lilies seemed real familiar.

Mighty Rahiem

About the Author

Mighty Rahiem is a deep-state agent; a CIA stooge.
He enjoys hiking, fly fishing and destabilizing fictitious
countries with his cyclotron.

More from Mighty Rahiem

and Zerthbooks.com

Available Now!

At Amazon.com andZerthbooks.com